William Richards

On the Road to Rome

and how two brothers got there

William Richards

On the Road to Rome
and how two brothers got there

ISBN/EAN: 9783337381837

Printed in Europe, USA, Canada, Australia, Japan

Cover: Foto ©Andreas Hilbeck / pixelio.de

More available books at **www.hansebooks.com**

ON THE ROAD TO ROME,

AND

How Two Brothers Got There.

BY

WILLIAM RICHARDS.

NEW YORK, CINCINNATI, CHICAGO:

BENZIGER BROTHERS,

Printers to the Holy Apostolic See.

1895.

INTRODUCTORY.

IN the Fall of 1886 it was arranged at one of the weekly meetings of Carroll Institute, in Washington City, D. C., that addresses should be given from time to time by members of the Institute, presenting reminiscences of the Catholic Church in the State from which the speaker came. As I was a native of Ohio, it fell to me to treat the subject with reference to that State. Accordingly I prepared an address which I delivered before the Institute on the evening of January 6, 1887. Subsequently the Institute, responding to the effort to raise funds for the BROWNSON monument, invited me to repeat the address. I cheerfully ac-

3

cepted the invitation out of devotion to
the memory of BROWNSON; and accordingly, on the evening of March 20, 1887,
I repeated the address with considerable
additions. It is now offered to the public
substantially in the form as last delivered,
though with some verbal changes, and
some additions, the most of which will
be found appended in notes.

WASHINGTON, D. C., March 10, 1895.

ON THE ROAD TO ROME.

AN ADDRESS.

MR. PRESIDENT, LADIES AND GENTLEMEN:

When on a former occasion I read a portion of this address before Carroll Institute, I explained that I could not, as requested, give any " Reminiscences of the Catholic Church in Ohio" — my native State—because it had so happened that I had never entered a Catholic church but once before I accepted the faith, and soon thereafter had emigrated to Keokuk, Iowa, and therefore my reminiscences had to partake more of a personal than a local nature, and would more properly be entitled: How and Why I Became a

Catholic. This title indicates what many of you know, that I was not born a Catholic.

It was my lot to be born and brought up in the small village of Granville, in central Ohio, which with one or two adjoining townships had been settled in 1805 by a colony of about one hundred families, who were mostly emigrants from the town of Granville, Mass. The majority of them were sturdy believers in the Westminster Catechism, and worthy descendants of New England Puritans — honest, sober, industrious, and thrifty, their religion being deeply pervaded by the sourness of Calvinism. It followed that I imbibed their views, feelings, and prejudices, and was not furnished with any instruction or traditions that were favorable to Roman Catholics. As a schoolboy, the first thing put into my hands was the " Little Primer," from which children learned their A B C's in such couplets as: "In Adam's fall, We sinned all," illustrated by a large letter A and a small picture of Adam, and similar couplets for every letter in the alphabet, which were easily learned and rarely forgotten.

I mention this primer because I retain a vivid remembrance of its thrilling picture of the so-called Protestant martyr, John Rogers, tied to a stake, standing in the midst of flames rising from a pile of blazing fagots, and gazed upon by his persecutors, and also by his weeping wife, who stood there, as the legend read, "with nine small children and one at the breast." This terrible scene was given as an awful example of the persecuting tyranny of that English queen whom the Protestants called "Bloody Mary." In the contemplation of that soul-harrowing picture, and the short story explaining it, it was natural that the youthful mind should conceive a vague horror of Catholics and their religion.

Connected with that early period of my life is another reminiscence which left its indelible impression. One day the startling report flew through our town and county as on the wings of the wind—for the telegraph was not then thought of—that one Peter Diamond, living in the woods, some four or five miles south of our village, had got into a fight and killed his man. This in itself was horrifying in a law-abiding community, where even justifiable homicide had scarcely ever been known to occur. But when it was eagerly told, though with bated breath, that Peter Diamond was a Papist and, before the affray, had actually gone to the adjoining county of Perry — where the Dominicans had a house at Somerset—and had paid a Roman Catholic priest for permission to commit this murder, getting pardon for the sin in advance, perhaps you can imagine the horror it inspired.*

And yet I seem to remember how the question rose and silently worked in my youthful mind: "Can it be possible that anybody can teach or believe in pardon for future sin, or believe that Almighty God will ratify such an arrangement at the judgment day?" Of course, I got no answer then, but continued for many years to have false views and bitter prej-

---

*Peter Diamond was tried, convicted, and sentenced to be hung, and when, on the day appointed (October 14, 1825), he stood on the scaffold, at Newark, with the rope round his neck, the Deputy Sheriff appeared at the last moment from Columbus, pushing his way through the crowd on his foaming steed, waving the reprieve of the Governor, much to the disappointment of the thousands of people who had gathered in from four or five surrounding counties to witness the hanging.

udices against Roman Catholics instilled into my mind by all my surroundings. When I recall the subtle and powerful influences of such early teachings, I am not surprised that both men and women who have been subjected to them are so slow to believe that there is anything in Catholic teachings worthy of their attention.

In the days that I am now recalling, so firmly was the conviction imbedded in the minds of Protestants that Catholic doctrines were full of error, and the Catholic Church itself a corrupt and moribund or played-out institution, that even those of them who became dissatisfied "Seekers after Truth" scarcely ever thought of looking in that direction to find a solution of the tremendous questions of human life that were perplexing and agitating their troubled souls. And the mischief was aggravated by the fact that such men as Carlyle, Emerson, Alcott, and various others who became leaders of thought in the non-Catholic world, confidently assumed and seemed never to suspect otherwise than that the hard absurdities of Calvinism and the other erroneous, incomplete, ridiculous, and illogical developments of Protestantism were genuine, orthodox Christianity. And this remark applies with equal force to men of a later date, such as Huxley and Ingersoll, whose names I mention because they are about my age, and are examples of men who had bigger doses of Calvinistic diet in their early days than I had, and unfortunately have not found or accepted the antidote as I did. It seems almost incredible that men of such general intelligence, and with such opportunities of finding the truth as they have, should so utterly fail to discover that the perversities of Protestantism are

not genuine Christianity.   And it is this
thought that should inspire all Catholics
with charity for those misguided people,
even including Ingersoll, and urge us to
make earnest and constant prayers for
their enlightenment.   I know from sad
experience that a person brought up in
the midst of such influences as I have indicated must inevitably be covered, as it
were, with almost inexpugnable encase-
ments, from which all the batteries of
argument and logic rebound and roll off
like water from the back of a duck in a
rainstorm.   How any human being es-
capes from such an environment, and
succeeds in making his way back into
the bosom of Mother Church, is a question the answer to which is generally full
of interest to Catholics, and especially to
converts.

Trusting to your kind indulgence, I
propose to say a few words relating to

my own experience in this regard. And
to begin with, it may seem to you a little
curious that probably the first step
towards my return to the Old Church,
and that of my elder brother, Henry L.
Richards, was taken when the minister
of our meeting—for we did not then say
church—the Rev. Ahab Jinks, allowed
carpenters and plasterers to work in fin-
ishing his dwelling-house on the *Sabbath-day*, his justification being that he
was obliged to give up his hired house
in a few days, and as winter was at hand
he feared to lose a single working hour
lest freezing weather should delay the
work and prevent the occupation of the
house at the stipulated time. With the
Puritan notion of the awful and solemn
sacredness of the Sabbath-day, which
stopped all work, and would not allow
children to play or even laugh aloud,
from sundown on Saturday night to sun-

down on Sunday night, you can imagine what commotion it caused in that congregation when it was known that the minister was a Sabbath-breaker! A majority of men and women in the meeting censured the minister, and insisted that he should retire. But there was a respectable minority who recognized the necessity of the minister's action, and justified it on scripture grounds. The controversy became hot and raged for months, and furnished a striking example of the anarchy that must result when every member of a society or congregation asserts his own right to interpret the scriptures, and lay down the law, and become a Pope for every other member.

It was the utter lack of authority in this disturbance which led my father,* who

---

* Dr. William Samuel Richards, born in New London, Conn., January 1, 1787, settled in Granville in 1811, and died there May 8, 1852.

supported the minister, to study the question of church government. The result
was that he preferred the order and seem-
ing authority of the Episcopal form of
church government to the Congregational
system based on irresponsible individualism, and he became an Episcopalian.
Perhaps a dozen other heads of families,
including the deposed minister, joined
him in organizing an Episcopal church in
1827. I recall the fact that he and his
friends were subsequently confirmed in
their choice by reading a little book published in 1832, entitled " An Apology for
the Episcopal Church," by Thomas S.
Brittan, which, as I now remember it,
contained the Catholic argument in support of Episcopacy, so far as it went.
My interest in this change consisted principally in the fact that we children were
no longer required to wrestle with the
dry and crabbed and forbidding pages of

the Westminster Smaller Catechism, in which I had just reached that long and awful paragraph on Predestination; but, greatly to my joy and relief, were put to study the more simple and practical catechism in the Episcopal Prayer Book.

I may say here, what of course I did not know then, that this Prayer Book was taken from the English Book of Common Prayer, which, in its Thirty-Nine Articles and Forms of Service, was the result of a compromise between various parties holding the opinions of Churchmen, Calvinists, Lutherans, and others; and it contained in its Articles of Religion, its Catechism, its Offices of Baptism, Confirmation, Communion, etc., a double set of principles—one set being Catholic and logically leading back to the Catholic Church from which they were derived, and the other set being radically Protestant, and, in the denial of Catholic truths, leading logically to the denial of all authority and all faith. No doubt some of you are aware of the interesting fact that Cardinal Newman and his talented and learned brother, who were at first evangelical or extremely low church members of the Established Church of England, separated in course of time— John Henry, the Cardinal, following the Catholic set of principles into the Catholic Church, and William Francis following the Protestant set into the denial of all faith. As I now recall the subtle power of the Protestant influences that surrounded and acted upon us every moment of our lives, it seems to me little less than a miracle that my brother and I ever got out of the fogs of darkness and doubt, and were at last brought into the glorious light of the grand old Catholic and Apostolic Church.

Another very important result of my

father's change was that my brother,
who, at an early age, had "experienced
religion," as they called it in the Congregational meeting of our village, decided to study for the Episcopal ministry,
and with that end in view went to Kenyon College, an Episcopal institution at
Gambier, Ohio, founded by Bishop Philander Chase, where I joined him, and
where we were graduated in the same
class (1838). I can safely say that during our college course we heard very little about, and nothing favorable to, the
Catholic Church.   Afterward, however,
while my brother was studying theology
at the theological seminary at Gambier,
there began to be discussions of the questions that divided low from high churchmen, and the latter from "Romanists."
Upon being ordained, it was his fortune
to be settled in a short time in Columbus, Ohio (1842), as the pastor of a high-

church congregation, which, by the way, was almost the only one of the kind in the State. There the standard works and arguments of the high church party became familiar to him through the zeal and kindness of his principal parishioner, Mr. Isaac N. Whiting, the well-known bookseller and publisher at Columbus; and as my brother was an honest-minded and logical seeker after truth, the progress which he made in the right direction was somewhat rapid, and in the end he went considerably further than his high church friends expected or desired.

While my brother was thus running his course as a theologian and successful pastor of a parish, it was my fortune to follow a quite different course in pursuit of philosophy, history, political science, law, and practical politics. It is not necessary, and I do not intend, to inflict upon you my biography. Yet it will be convenient to allude now and then to a prominent fact or event that may, as it were, be used as a peg on which to hang a sign indicating my progress to Rome— though, of course, I had then no more notion of going to Rome than I had of going to the moon.   And thus it seems pertinent to mention that while I was making an extra course of study at my *alma mater*, principally under the instruction of the Rev. Dr. William Sparrow, from Ireland—a learned and talented man, and a most competent and thorough teacher, though a radical Protestant—it so happened that there was a "revival" among the students.   It commenced without preparation or special efforts—no one knew how.   The first convert was a young student from Virginia, named Kinsolving—his conversion from a rather wild and irreligious life having been so sudden and remarkable as to attract attention. He is now (1887) a prominent Episcopal minister in Virginia. Beginning in this way, the revival went on until nearly every student was counted as a "convert." The last month or two of the college year (1839) was given up mainly to this revival, as the saving of souls was considered of vastly more importance than mere learning or any other earthly interest.

I allude to this event, and mention the fact that I was one of the subjects, simply for the purpose of setting before you what was, and perhaps still is, the evangelical notion of "getting religion." "Seekers" were diligently impressed with the notion that they must expect, seek, and pray for a "change of heart." And when, after a sharp struggle, sometimes short, and sometimes lasting days or weeks, one could at last get up in meeting and say with tears of joy, or without, but with evident sincerity, that, "at such an hour and such a place—possibly behind a big log in the woods, or in the loft of the barn, or in the closet if he had one, or elsewhere—while agonizing and praying to the Lord, suddenly he was convicted, light came in upon his soul, and he felt happy," then he was regarded and received as a convert. He had "experienced religion"; he was no longer a mere worldling; he had come out from the world; the old Adam was put off; old things had passed away, and all things had become new! While the excitement of the revival lasted, there was a happy state of *feeling*. But it is not in the nature of man to keep up such excitement continuously.* In time, the tension

---

* I remember that there was one young man there who had the good judgment to avoid all such excitement, and who said to himself, "This is the most important matter that ever will or can engage my at-

must give way, and lassitude and cold-
ness follow. Then came in many cases
the surprising and painful discovery that
the "change of heart" was not a radical

---

tention, and I must decide it with a cool, calm
judgment." And he very soon decided that it was the
highest wisdom "to turn unto the Lord," and he did
so, and he proved to be one of the most straightfor-
ward, sensible, and zealous converts that I knew.
Perhaps I may be pardoned for mentioning the case
of another young man, who, greatly to my surprise,
was brought to me, by a very zealous and pious
church member, to receive instruction. I was very
free to give him my views, and was afterward com-
plimented by an old church member and a competent
judge, who overheard my instructions (without my
knowledge), and pronounced them good. But I noticed that my pupil, though a good listener, said very
little, and I never heard that he was "converted,"
though I did hear of him till the day of his death as
a most excellent and conscientious man, a regular at-
tendant at church, and always having a profound
sense of right and of his duty to God. My theory of
his case was that, with his cool judgment and correct
conduct of life, he did not see the necessity or the use
of going through the excitement that took hold of
nearly every one of the converts. The name of the
young man was Rutherford B. Hayes, afterward
President of the United States.

change after all—that the old man Adam was *not* conquered and put off, and that it was still just as easy as of old to be wicked, to get angry, to lie, or swear, or slander, to have bad thoughts, or be worldly-minded.

And the convert who held on for a time was not without difficulties. For he was sure to be plied with the doctrine of *total* depravity, and "justification by faith alone;" and he would hear the zealous preacher declare that "the whole head was sick and the whole heart faint," and that one could not "think a good thought or do a good deed," or if he did they would count for nothing, for he could not be saved by works, but by faith in the Saviour, whose merits would be "imputed" to him for righteousness which would envelop his "total depravity" as with a white robe of purity. And then a reflective man would begin to think that if he was *totally* depraved it would be folly to expect that radical change which he had been taught to look for. And so, when the reaction came, as it did with multitudes, the painful question would arise: "Was I converted? If there had been a real 'change of heart' would I now be in this cold, unsatisfactory state?" To make a long story short, a majority or a large number of converts, wherever and whenever the revival occurred in those days, would generally become "backsliders," and very many of them would come to be counted among the reprobate or the unregenerate.

How did I escape that result? The answer to that question is closely connected with the story of my progress to Rome. Before and after the revival interlude, I was making with Dr. Sparrow a diligent study of Cousin's lectures on the "History of Philosophy," his "Criti-

cism of Locke on the Understanding,"
and Dr. Lieber's "Political Ethics." I
am not going to dwell upon the world of
new ideas—grand and absorbing—which
these studies opened up to me. For my
present purpose it will suffice to recall
Cousin's famous scheme of eclecticism,
that is to say, of culling and selecting
from each one of the numerous systems
of philosophy its particular and un-
doubted truth, and by skilfully putting
together these various truths, construct-
ing a harmonious whole, and calling it
eclectic philosophy. I well remember
how this suggested to me the ingenious
scheme of selecting from each of the
numerous Protestant sects that portion of
truth which it held, and thus putting together a collection of truths and practices
which should be altogether free from
error, and would constitute true Christianity. Was it not a brilliant scheme?

You may at once infer from this that I had some difficulties about what constituted the true faith, which were considerably increased when my reaction came on, though, thanks to the faithful teachings and good examples of my parents, I could not give up my belief in God; and I had a vague sort of conviction that there must be some truth in the scheme of redemption if we could only get at it. But how to get at it was the question. Thus it was that the great question of authority began to loom up. How many years it was in taking definite shape in my mind and coming to a head, remains to be stated.

A very important part of my course with Dr. Sparrow was, as already mentioned, the study of Dr. Francis Lieber's great and celebrated work on "Political Ethics," which came from the press late in 1838, and for a number of years held its place at the head of works on political science. Time will permit me on this occasion to mention only two ideas or views which I obtained from that work, and which radically influenced the formation of my solutions of certain great problems of the day.

The first was Dr. Lieber's complete refutation of that absurd theory, so much dwelt upon by Blackstone in his Commentaries, and by others in their discussions of the origin of the State, that the primitive condition of man was a "state of nature" or mere savagism—a state or condition in which poor, ignorant savages lived without law or organized government, in solitary and gloomy equality —the only government being that by club-law, or the law of the strongest. Erroneous as this theory was, yet philosophers had not then (1839–40) developed the still lower, more erroneous, and

more absurd theory—so widely accepted
by the so-called scientists of this day—
that man originated in protoplasm, and
after an indefinitely long period of time
was gradually evolved through the mol-
lusk into the tadpole, and from the tadpole through various changes into the
monkey, and from the monkey through
other changes into the poor, ignorant
savage. The nearest approach to that
kind of science was, as I remember, the
fanciful speculation of Lord Monboddo—
which was received with incredulous
laughter — that the monkey, by sitting
on his tail, had gradually worn it down
to a short stump, and while doing so
had chattered himself into the savage
man.

But unfortunately the Blackstone theory of man in a "state of nature," out of
which he slowly emerged through bar-
barism by successive steps of improve-

ment, until he reached the highest civili-
zation of the ancient nations, has left its
mark upon nearly all the literature of the
world for the last hundred years or more.
It was this theory that Dr. Lieber at-
tacked with vigor and successfully controverted, showing that there never had
been such a condition as that imaginary
"state of nature"—that man, as Montes-
quieu said, is born in society and there
must ever remain; that society was of
divine origin equally with the individual man, and that it was ordained
from the beginning that man should
work out his destiny in this world, and
for the next, only in and through society.

This was the first idea which I learned
from Dr. Lieber, and the second was simply its logical development.   For society,
with its divine origin, necessarily culmi-
nated in the State.   And, therefore, the

State is not, in its origin, a voluntary association of savages who have become tired of club-law; nor is it a co-partnership of shareholders to promote each one's selfish interest; nor an immense insurance company established for the protection of property, and incidentally "to look out that my neighbor does not pick my pocket" or cut my throat; nor a cunningly devised machine to grind out taxes and support the constable and the gallows. It is neither one nor all of these. For the State is aboriginal with man, and, jurally considered, is the society of societies in the temporal order, having an organic life of its own, which, in its identity and continuity, is distinct and palpable like that of the individual man. The individual, indeed, is above the State in that he is not limited to time, but is made to be a citizen of eternity. But then the State is above the individual because, being the organism of society, it never dies, but lives on from age to age, embracing and sustaining all generations of men in their unbroken continuity.

Now both of these ideas were of immense benefit to me in many ways—the first one by guarding me against the errors of any teacher or any book whose starting point and fundamental assumption was that the primitive condition of man was that of the low and ignorant savage; for the theories on the origin of society, government, language, and religion, flowing from such a source, are certain to be mixed up with very serious and dangerous errors;—the only true theory being that in the beginning God made the heavens and the earth, and in due time ushered man into life, a grand and glorious being, whose nature, being fashioned in body and soul upon the idea of the Incarnate Son,* as Father Faber said, "was beautiful in its perfection, but was clothed upon by the surpassing beauty of primeval grace and the radiance of original justice," and "the greatness of whose science was such that we can hardly form an idea of it to ourselves," while "the most startling miracles of the saints are but feeble indications and partial recoveries of that rightful and supernatural dominion over nature which man possessed and exercised" in his first estate, but whose sad and mournful history from the time of the fall down to the Christian era was one of gradual departure from God's truth as given in the primitive revelation, involving loss of

---

* For whom He foreknew, He also predestinated to be made conformable to the image of His Son : that He might be the first-born amongst many brethren. —Rom. viii. 29.

And God said : Let us make man to Our image. —Gen. i. 26.

3

control of the powers of nature, and more
or less rapid decline in religion, in morals,
in language, in art, in government, and,
in short, in everything that was good and
true and beautiful.

And, secondly, immense benefit was
derived from familiarizing the mind with
the idea that society is a living organism, an organized body, having an organic life of its own, with a head, an
office, a mission, as distinct as that of the
individual.   Those of you who have
never had the misfortune of having been
Protestants can scarcely conceive of the
difficulty which Protestants had, in the
days of which I am speaking, of forming
to themselves any notion of the State or
the Church as an organized body.   Their
congregations were simply meetings of
individuals, each one asserting the unlimited right of private judgment, and
their religious teachings being addressed

to each one as if he had merely a *spiritual* nature—"the scheme of redemption," or atonement, or *at-one-ment*, as Dr. Albert Barnes called it in his Commentaries, being a scheme which did not necessarily call for the coming of a redeemer in the *body*—the only use they made of that fact being the sentimental one of appealing to our feelings in view of the great humility of the Redeemer in taking upon Himself the form of man, and voluntarily suffering the pains and agonies of the crucifixion. This came to appear to me to be mere sentimentalism, and I was puzzled by the speculations of some Unitarians who held that we have nothing but a historical Christianity, which we can criticise at pleasure; while we may, indeed, if we choose, indulge an unbounded admiration for "the Christ" as a great and good and really wonderful historical person who lived nearly two thousand years ago!

I had not then learned the profound truth that the Church is a continuous, ever-living, and teaching body, with all that that implies, and especially always having the Body and Blood of Our Lord ever present upon the altar, ever giving life to the humble and penitent communicant. But, of course, it took me yet some years to see it in that light, though I readily perceive now how the ideas I gained from Lieber and Brownson on organized society, and the views on the incarnation which I had subsequently read in the writings of Hugh Davey Evans in "The True Catholic," were what Coleridge called "seed-thoughts" which took root and finally bore glorious fruit. In the mean time, however, other influences were working.

Thus I find an old memorandum which reminds me that while studying law at the Yale Law School in 1842, I became profoundly interested in Carlyle's book on "Heroes, Hero-Worship, and the Heroic in History." I never have forgotten the surprise with which I read that passage in his lecture on "The Hero as Priest," wherein, after glorifying Luther and the Reformation, he started the question whether "popery" would ever come back again, speaking very contemptuously of the "Poor old Popehood" as if it were nearly dead, and giving his answer in this oracular manner, to wit: "The poor old Popehood will not die away entirely, as Thor has done, for some time yet; nor ought it. We may say, the Old never dies till this happen: Till all the soul of good that was in it have got itself transfused into the practical New. While a good work remains capable of being done by the Romish form; or, what is inclusive of all, while a *pious life* remains capable of being led by it, just so long, if

we consider, will this or the other human
soul adopt it, go about as a living witness of it.   So long it will obtrude itself
on the eye of us who reject it till we in
our practice too have appropriated whatsoever of truth was in it.   Then, but also
not till then, it will have no charm more
for any man.   The Romish form lasts
here for a purpose.   Let it last as long
as it can."

How judicial, how oracular, how con-
descending!   But such was then Carlyle's authority with me that this remark
worked a small revolution in my Protestant notion that the Roman Catholic
Church was so filled with erroneous doctrine and corrupt practices that no soul
need expect to find salvation there.
Thenceforth, however, I no longer
doubted that a "pious life" might be
lived in that Church so as to secure salvation hereafter.   This admission once

made, you can readily infer that the process of softening prejudice went on apace, though it was rather slow in its operation.

Here would be the place, if I had the time, and you the patience to listen, to set forth at some length the results of the diligent study which I made during the years 1842–43–44 of Carlyle's brilliant and soul-stirring essays, which spoke to me like the blast of a bugle in the stirring battle of life, and of his "Sartor Resartus," his "Past and Present," and his "French Revolution," in all of which he exposed and riddled the shams of modern society, and especially exploded the modern commercial system, based as it is upon the utter selfishness of competition, and proclaiming as it does the modern Gospel of Mammon: "Every man for himself and the devil take the hindmost!" But I must hasten on and bespeak your

attention while I refer as briefly as possible to an incident which caused a sensa-
tion somewhat like unto the sudden
bursting of a bombshell in the tent of
the enemy.

In the summer of 1844, I was invited
by the faculty of Kenyon College to deliver an oration at their ensuing commencement. Accepting this invitation,
I spent some weeks in carefully preparing an oration in which I discussed and
reviewed the signs of the times, and set
forth what appeared to me to be the pre-
vailing tendencies of the age in its social,
political, and religious aspects. In doing
this I availed myself freely of the studies
which, during the preceding five years,
I had made of Cousin, Lieber, Carlyle,
and Brownson—and as to the latter I may
say, in passing, that his essays on syn-
thetic philosophy, and his profound discussions of the political questions grow-

ing out of the Dorr rebellion in Rhode Island, all of which appeared in the *Democratic Review* in 1842–43, had greatly interested me, and led me to take and read his *Quarterly Review*, which he resumed in 1844 upon his disagreement with the editor of the *Democratic Review*. Brownson's views substantially agreed with those of Dr. Lieber on the origin of society, the constitution of the State, and the true theory of constitutional government, which I made use of freely in my oration in combating what I considered to be the rapid tendency of that day toward Democratic absolutism, as shown by the persistent attempts to break down the intermediary, or, as Lieber called them, the mediatorial institutions, such as the free law-making representative, the unawed jury, the executive governed by law instead of his own will, the independent judiciary, and other like institutions,

which were the growth of Christian civil-
ization, and which should stand between
the supreme power of the State and the
subject or individual, insuring the safe
generation, expression, and transmission
by the legislature of the public will in the
shape of public law, to be wisely interpreted by the judiciary, and firmly but
legally executed by the executive branch
—thus avoiding the tyranny of absolutism on the one hand, and the disruption
of unrestrained individualism on the
other hand; and thus, by insuring the
harmonious co-existence of order and liberty, solving what Carlyle called the
hugest problem of modern times.

I may also say that, progressing in en-
tire sympathy with my brother in his
theological studies, I had with him become a high churchman, and so we had
begun to lay much stress upon the doctrines of apostolical succession, baptismal

regeneration, the real presence, and that assertion in one of the Thirty-nine Articles "that the Church hath authority in controversies of faith." We had even come to admit that Luther's so-called Reformation was in fact no reformation, and that Protestantism was loaded down with sad and direful consequences. And yet we held that the Roman Church was overlaid with errors, while the Anglican Church—founded as we fondly fancied by St. Paul himself—was a pure reformed church!

Some of you may remember that just at that time (1844), Episcopalians were in the highest tension of excitement growing out of the agitation of those church questions, and the publication in England of the celebrated "Tracts for the Times," including the famous "Tract Number XC," in which Dr. John Henry Newman undertook to reconcile the stand-

ards of faith of the English Church with
the creed of Pope Pius IV. This excitement had been greatly intensified in February, 1843, by Dr. Newman's formal re-
tractation of the charges which he had
uttered against the Church of Rome and,
in the September following, giving up
his living and resigning his office as a
clergyman, though he was not received
into the Catholic Church until October 9,
1845. Bishop McIlvaine, of Ohio—the
great gun of the low church party in the
United States—had added fuel to the
flames by publishing his book against
"Oxford Divinity."

Under these circumstances I appeared
at the Commencement of 1844, which was
presided over by Bishop McIlvaine, and
was attended by many of the clergy and
prominent laymen of the diocese of Ohio,
and by a large crowd of visitors. I ven-
tured to proclaim church views and theo-

ries quite antagonistic to theirs, though it is proper to say that I began, and spent some time, as already indicated, in pointing out some dangerous and revolutionary tendencies in political and social matters—which views met, perhaps, with general acceptance, as nearly all of us were Whigs of the Henry Clay school.

But my principal effort was, following the teachings of Carlyle, to show the horrible results of that famous doctrine of "competition and laissez faire" introduced and advocated by the French economists, and adopted and published in England by Adam Smith, Malthus, Ricardo, Paley, and Bentham. I summed up this doctrine by saying: "Its fundamental principle or starting point was 'the greatest happiness of the greatest number.' This general result was to be obtained by each one 'pursuing his own true and substantial happiness' in his

own way. Wherefore, each one should
have the 'largest liberty,' be 'let alone'
to come and go as he pleased—to buy and
sell where and what and how he pleased.
'Enlightened self-interest' would teach
him to respect the law of *meum* and *tuum*,
and, in seeking a particular, to promote
the general result. Competition would
be the life of business, or 'the soul of
trade,' and straighten out occasional ir-
regularities. And for the rest, the great
law of 'supply and demand' would regu-
late all, and thus restore the lost Eden to
earth! Was it not," I exclaimed, intend-
ing to be sarcastic, "a beautiful theory, a
fascinating vision, worthy of all accepta-
tion among men?"

And then I controverted the ultimate
fact of this theory that man must be
happy, by declaring with Carlyle that the
fact of nature is that man is not born to
be happy here, but is sent into this world

to do his duty and get his proper work done. Then, after showing with many more words that the fundamental assumption of this teaching was false, I alleged that the whole theory in practice goes wrong, and then followed a paragraph which, on account of its applicability to the present time, though written over forty-two years ago, I think you will pardon me for repeating. I said:

"And besides, *'enlightened'* self-interest is found to be scarce. The 'demand' for it, indeed, is great; while ever an abundant 'supply' of mere selfishness remains, to clash and jar and compete with self-interest as best it may. With all possible compensatory adjustments, with all conceivable checks and balances, by the 'never so cunning mechanizing of self-interests' [though the ingenious device of substituting the bell-punch and such like cunning mechanical contrivances in the place of sterling integrity had not then been thought of], your 'laws of supply and demand' and 'laissez faire,' it is found, do not feed the hungry, clothe the naked, restrain the all-absorbing greed of gain and lust of power. Nor yet, as Carlyle said, do they solve the problem from which they started, and which they undertook to solve: 'Given a world of knaves, to educe an honesty from their united action!' In short, universal 'laissez faire' and competition, we discover, finally turn out to be: Universal liberty to cut yourself loose from all men and seek your own interest; to suspect all men; liberty, therefore, to drive cute bargains with Yankee shrewdness, or else liberty to die by honest starvation. 'Laissez faire!' 'Let me alone!' 'Give me independence!' so long clamored in the world, result at last in establishing— not merely in the commercial world—but one relation between men, that of cash-payment! Every one for himself and due payment of wages in money; 'cash the sole nexus of man to man;' this being your highest code of morality, is it at all astonishing, if, instead of beholding the lost Eden restored, we catch no uncertain glimpses of the mean perplexities of society, with its fraud and deceptions, its shams, its vulpine cunning and clashing interests, its winkings and blinkings at dishonesty and rascality?"

And yet, my friends, let me say, in passing, that in those days (1844) the ingenious money-making business of wrecking railroads, and virtually stealing them from the first subscribers to the stock, had hardly begun; nor had speculators yet entered upon the equally ingenious and disreputable scheme of "watering" the stocks of great companies; nor had the sense of morality and fair dealing be-

4

tween man and man become so benumbed
and depraved as to tolerate dealing in
"futures;" and as to that diabolical speculation in breadstuffs and other neces-
saries of human subsistence, in which
one gambler pretends to buy what he
does not want from another gambler who
does not own and cannot deliver it—*that*
was still an unheard-of atrocity. Nor
was there then a small army of default-
ing trustees and bank presidents and
cashiers and "boodle" aldermen migrat-
ing in rapid succession to the cities of
refuge in Canada and elsewhere. Nor
were there any enormous corporations
stretching from ocean to ocean, combin-
ing and "pooling their issues" in order to
escape the disastrous consequences of
ruinous competition, and laying a heavy
hand upon the whole business of a help-
less community in order to fill their own
coffers with their stealings. Nor yet

were there any gigantic industrial companies which, in order to increase their disproportionate gains, were importing ignorant and half-starved Italians and Bohemians and the "heathen Chinee," to work for half wages, and displace and reduce to starvation the laborers of our own land.

And yet the results of competition in those days were truly bad enough, especially in England, as they were vividly described by Carlyle; and they were already appearing even in this glorious country, where economists had begun to stigmatize the unsuccessful laborer as a "pauper" and cast him into the poorhouse—that wretched abode over whose portals the sad and gloomy legend should be written: "Whoso enters here leaves hope behind!" Even then the good old common law described by Blackstone as to forestalling the market, regrating, and engrossing (which were indictable and finable offences), was almost a dead letter, or in modern phrase had about reached the point of "innocuous desuetude"; and, finally, men were beginning, in reply to the searching question: "Where is thy brother?" to give an answer like that of Cain: "My brother? Am I my brother's keeper? Have I not paid him his wages in cash? I have no further *business* with him!"

And so I said on that commencement day at Gambier: "The competitive system is making its ultimate manifestation in some all-too-common vagrant Sam Slick, who, friendless, unrelated, roves over the earth, doing strokes of trade, without brother, without home, the incarnation of Individualism. Well may we ask," I said, "whither are we tending? What kind of a society is that 'where there is no longer any true social idea extant'—not even an idea of a common home, but only of a common lodging-house and merchants' exchange,—where friendship, communion, is an incredible tradition, and love of thy neighbor only a thing to be *preached* of on Sunday!"

But this "final outcome of the 'greatest happiness' principle, or utilitarian theory, was," I said, "the last wave of the movement started by the French economists in the eighteenth century"—one of its products being the terrible French Revolution, which Carlyle characterized as a new assertion of man's rights, a terrific protest against shams—"proclamation of a truth once more, though a truth clad in hell-fire!" and I quoted the philosophic historian as maintaining that this revolution was not an isolated fact, but stands connected with and related to the whole past, as well as to the whole future, and that, with the rebellions and revolutions in England, "it found its point of departure in the Reformation of Luther." And thus having traced the modern Gospel of Mammon, with its un-restrained individualism, its competition and pauperism,* and the destructive

---

*A striking evidence of reaction against the in-human selfishness practised in commercial life and defended by heartless economists was presented by Prof. Felix Adler in his lecture on February 14, 1895, in the School of Applied Ethics, at the Columbian University, Washington, D. C., when, among other weighty utterances, he said, as reported in the *Post*:

ABJECT MISERY ON ALL SIDES.

"I will criticise this principle of selfishness on the ground of its actual results. We see abject misery every day in spite of the vast fortunes accumulated side by side with it; we see the audacity of our trusts, the heartless desertion of public interest on the part of the wealthiest, the shirking of the bur-dens of taxation on the part of those best able to bear it, and the oppression of those least able to bear it."

He had previously said, as reported :

"There are, in my estimation, two ways in which the ethical student and worker can speed the moral development of industrial society of the present day. Assuming as a fact that men in their commercial life

revolutions of three centuries back to the Reformation, I exclaimed before my audience that day:

"Given your protest against *spiritual* abuses in the sixteenth century, your protest against the existence of sacred rights between rulers and ruled in the seventeenth century, your protest against

---

are largely governed by selfishness, it would be the function of the ethical student to consider what checks can be imposed upon that selfishness and what new conditions can be prescribed to soften the harshness of economic egotism. The second function would be to consider whether in the nature of things it is necessary that selfishness should always be the leading motive of the commercial and industrial life of man, and whether there are not other motives by which the world can live that would not dangerously affect production, distribution, and consumption; that would not lessen the industrial efficiency of mankind, but at the same time elevate the tone of those who are engaged in industrial and commercial life."

If the School of Applied Ethics persistently follows out this line of thought to its logical conclusion, may we not hope to see it achieving great success in bringing back the civilized, otherwise designated as

all restraint and all authority in the
eighteenth century, and the protest
against the existence of any relation
between men but that of cash-payment
in the nineteenth century is also given.
Did the one necessarily contain the
other? Perhaps not. But *from* the one
to the other we are tugged along by a

---

the devilized, world to the salutary practice of the
Golden Rule as taught by Pope Leo XIII., wherein is
the sole remedy for the fearful evils that threaten
speedy revolution and widespread disruption?

Is it not an encouraging sign of the times that, on
February 28, 1895, at the regular Thursday afternoon
lecture of the Catholic University, Washington,
D. C., the Hon. Carroll D. Wright, Commissioner of
Labor, after alluding to what Carlyle called the dis-
mal science, said: "There is a new and better school
of political economy in which the old question of
'will it pay' gives place to the more pertinent question, 'is it right;'" and he held "firmly to the view
that the Ten Commandments and the Golden Rule,
faithfully applied by all conditions of society, would
go a long way toward reconciling the differences between capital and labor," adding that "there is no
safer platform for employer and employee, even on
the plane of expediency, than the Decalogue."

chain that snaps not nor breaks in any link.

"Reform of whatsoever evil thing is upon earth," I added, "is forever a duty. Protest against error, falsehood, and tyranny is forever necessary. Only it behooves a man to think well of the spirit in which he will make it. If his protest is made in wrath and hatred, and with headlong selfish violence, it *may* become 'denial of divine right as well as diabolic wrong.' And then your denial of Mother Church becomes denial of the divine right of rulers—spiritual and temporal; passes into the mitigated form of Presbyterianism, matures into Congregationalism, goes to seed in Socinianism, and then, naturally flying off into innumerable independent, isolated, hostile fragments, ends in cold, horrible selfishness and ghastly despair."

Then briefly discussing the "right of

private judgment," I said: "Man's con-
science, his judgment, his belief are his
own, and by these he must stand or fall.
In this world of distraction and error,
what a man shall judge to be right and
good and true, what with all his heart to
believe—this is his highest difficulty—
how blessed if some highest, wisest mind
would teach him what."

Ah! my friends, what painful seeking
for guidance was therein expressed!
What doubts and "questionings of destiny" would have been saved me had
I then known the Infallible Church!
Thank God, that knowledge was to come.
But then, all I could say was this: "Private judgment, unchainable as the winds,
must be exercised. It exists forever a
sacred right to be exercised. But woe to
him who, casting away fear and rever-
ence, in the pride of intellect, or in the
obstinacy of ignorance, asserts this lib-

erty to the length of making his own will the supreme law, and his own selfish feelings his standard of right. There are limits here, perhaps undefinable, yet real, beyond which it is perilous for man to go, yet beyond which he has gone. 'I stand alone before my God' is a solemn truth; yet, not wholly, not lovingly understood, it leads to results injurious, in the spiritual world, to the highest and holiest relations of man to his fellows—results which we see all round us in life, harmonizing with the wretched results of 'universal competition and laissez faire.' "

And then I deprecated the radical conduct of those who " go on asserting this right of private judgment to the length of abolishing government with the 'No-government' man; of becoming a law to yourself with the Perfectionist; of finding in the pure reason the absolute God with the Transcendentalist; of making the absolute God the soul of the universe with the Pantheist; and, as the last act of this career, of plunging into the bottomless, wide, wasting whirlpool of Atheism." And then, referring to the rule of faith recognized by my audience, I concluded as follows:

"And now you will point me, as a refuge from all these distractions, to that ancient book, the Bible, as containing the ground plan of all life and duty, accompanying the act with the declaration: 'He is free whom the truth makes free.' And then, with Pilate of old, I ask 'What is truth?' And unlike him I *will* stay for an answer. Is that necessarily truth which one may believe with ever so much heartfelt sincerity? If so, then is not the sincere Perfectionist, walking with the Bible in his hand, right? Is not the Transcendentalist who, with awful sincerity, finds the Most High God in the pure reason, right? Is not every sectarian right who holds his particular view or opinion with sincerity? Are, then, truth and duty dependent upon the transitory feelings and perceptions of each finite individual? Or is it not most certain that truth is eternal, at one with itself, and possessing a harmonious diversity in unity? If this is certain, then does it necessarily follow that I, that any isolated individual, with his diseased will, innumerable prejudices, and warped feelings, will apprehend the whole truth?— for the question is not with how *little* truth I can possibly get along. Is it not becoming a very general feeling with men that each one's belief, formed, as it has been, by the unlimited exercise of the right of private judgment, and leading to the results already ·mentioned, needs verifying? And do they not feel that they cannot with safety appeal from their own unauthorized versions of truth to the versions of other isolated men equally unauthorized? Is it not becoming the earnest, passionate cry of the times: Where is the version that we can depend upon? Is it no longer possible to discover a manly, noble, god-like relation between men,—a principle which shall lead to a glorious unity in diversity, and bind men together once more in a true, loving, universal brotherhood?"

Such was the conclusion of my oration on that Commencement Day in August, 1844.* Do you ask how it was received,

---

*At the end of my speech, as I left the stage and walked down the aisle, I met my friend, Thomas Sparrow (brother of Dr. Sparrow, and then a lawyer in Columbus), going toward the stage to deliver the next oration. He saluted me with the blunt question: "What did you mean by that oration?" Having no time to answer fully, I simply replied: "I meant just what I said." "Well," said he, "I brought two orations with me—the best one is on French

and what was its effect? I can answer
only in a general way that it was the
topic of discussion that day at many of
the dinner-tables in Gambier; and you
will doubtless *not* be surprised to learn
that some of my hearers promptly said:
"That young man is well on the road to
Rome." But perhaps you *will* be surprised to hear that, while I was appar-

---

literature, and the other is on William Leggett, and
now I am going to give you a counterblast by reading the one on Leggett." And so he proceeded to
eulogize Leggett and shock the feelings of his Whig
auditors by uttering the most radical Democratic—
then called "Locofoco"—doctrines.

At the close of the exercises, as the people were
going out, the Rev. George Denison (my brother-
in-law, and my exceedingly low church pastor at
Newark), met me with the ejaculation: "Well, Tom
gave you a good counterblast, and I am glad of it.
Not that I am a Democrat." "Oh! no," said I,
"you are a Whig in politics, but unfortunately a
Locofoco in religion!" And then each went his way.
I heard that he was greatly annoyed by having to
admit, in answer to sundry questioners, that I came
from his parish.

ently so near to Rome, it took me yet nine more years to get there.* And this is the more surprising to myself now after again glancing over certain articles of Brownson's in his *Quarterly Review* for January, April, and July, 1844 — all of which I had read, and some of which I had carefully studied and even quoted from in preparing my oration.

Brownson, I may remind you, had at

---

* At this point my conclusion of this address, on its first reading before the Institute on January 6, 1887, was as follows :

"The story, however, of my final struggle and triumph must be written hereafter, if at all. And now making my apology for holding you so long, and returning you my thanks for your patient attention, I beg to suggest that, in view of the fact that the act of our village minister in 'breaking the Sabbath-day' resulted, under God, in bringing two brothers into the Church—the elder of whom has brought up a son who is now (1887) a Jesuit priest at Woodstock [in 1895 President of Georgetown University,] it would be a good and wholesome thought to pray for the soul of Ahab Jinks."

the close of 1843 severed his connection with the Unitarians, and come back again to Trinitarianism. The publication of this fact, and of certain essays of his on church questions, had attracted wide attention, and all those who were watching his career—and they were many—were curious to see where he would land. Prior to 1842 he had published and written most of the articles in the Boston *Quarterly Review*. In the latter part of 1842, that review having been discontinued, he wrote for the *Democratic Review* until the close of 1843, when, owing to a radical disagreement with the editor in discussions about the Dorr Rebellion in Rhode Island, he recommenced in January, 1844, the publication of his quarterly in Boston, calling it *Brownson's Quarterly Review*. In the July number he reviewed the letters of Bishop Hopkins, of Vermont, "On the Novelties which Disturb

5

Our Peace," in which Brownson advanced serious objections to Anglicanism. At that time Dr. Samuel Seabury was the great gun of the high churchmen in this country, and was the able editor of *The Churchman*—the organ of the high church party. In the hope of inducing Brownson to join the Episcopal Church, Dr. Seabury replied to his objections to Anglicanism, using his most powerful arguments. To these Brownson replied in his October number for 1844, demonstrating with unanswerable logic that the Anglican Church was schismatic, and announcing at its conclusion his conversion to Rome, being "happy," he said, "to acknowledge the authority of the Holy Father." Somehow this logical shot, which I shall notice further on, did not then demolish the armor with which I had covered myself. And so I quit taking his *Review*, much to my subsequent regret, and stuck to our high church, pet branch theory. And soon thereafter becoming involved in the distractions of business and practical politics, for several years I gave comparatively little attention to the studies which had hitherto been so deeply absorbing.

However, as the months and years passed on some incidents occurred which I recall with interest, and which may be mentioned as having had a certain influence in the development of my church views. The first of these to be mentioned in the order of time occurred while I was preparing my Kenyon oration. I remember one day (in 1844), while sitting in my law office in Newark, Ohio, with Major Benjamin W. Brice (afterward paymaster-general of the United States Army, and now, March, 1887, a resident of this city — Washington,

D.C.—* together with William D. Wilson and George Peyton Conrad, all lawyers, we engaged in the discussion of high church doctrines and Puseyism (the exciting topics of that time), and as I was known to be high church, I was asked to state what were the peculiar tenets of that school.   Having mentioned apostolical succession, baptismal regeneration, and the real presence, the discussion centred upon the latter topic, and became somewhat exciting, when Major Brice, who did not profess any religious belief in particular, though he attended the Episcopal Church, astonished us by saying, in regard to the Roman Catholic doctrine of Transubstantiation, that he could not see why one who believed that God became an infant in the womb of a virgin should have any difficulty in be-

---

* Died in December, 1892.

lieving that He was present in the Host. This was to me a startling way of putting the case. For, although I was a firm believer in the Incarnation, yet, as I recall it now, the truth as stated by Major Brice had never been presented to me in that realistic manner. But the idea took lodgment and abided with me. And I think you will appreciate my surprise when, some twelve years later, after I had become a Catholic and had migrated to Iowa, while absorbed one day in reading Father Faber's profound and wonderful work on "The Blessed Sacrament," I came to this sentence:

"Multitudes of men believe the Incarnation who disbelieve Transubstantiation; yet out of twenty arguments they will use against the last, the chances are that nineteen would lie equally against the first." And on the following page, referring to "the curious national frenzy

which took place [in England in 1851] in
consequence of the establishment of the
Catholic hierarchy in England," in 1850,
Father Faber mentions how "an infidel
journal observing upon the fact of Protestants chalking over the walls [in London]
'No Wafer Gods,' said that it seemed to
reasoning men who held themselves sub-
limely aloof from both parties, an absurd
inconsistency for those to make any serious objection to the Catholic who looks at
the Host and says it is God, who themselves require you to look into the face of
a new-born Babe and to believe It is the
Eternal and Immutable God!" You may
be sure, when I read that passage away
off in Iowa, I recalled with some interest
the remark of my friend, Major Brice,
made a dozen years before.

Another incident which I could never
forget was my first sight of Archbishop
Purcell. It may have been early in 1846

when the report was circulated among us that Bishop Purcell was coming to officiate at the Catholic church in Newark. Some five or six of us young lawyers, attracted by the fame of the bishop's celebrated controversy with Alexander Campbell, were anxious to see and hear him, and accordingly we went to the church at the appointed time. This was my first entrance into a Catholic church. What I saw on this occasion was the poorest specimen of a dull brick-and-mortar building, with a cold brick floor, plain, even rough, seats, a dim light, and a small congregation of poor Irish and Germans. It was a low Mass, though I did not then know one Mass from another, and had not the remotest idea what was going on about the altar, as I could hear nothing, and there was little to be seen except the dinginess of the walls and floors. It seemed to me a singular way to conduct public worship, for I did not then know that the priest was performing the highest act of worship by offering the unbloody sacrifice upon the altar of God, thus fulfilling the prophecy of Malachy that "from the rising of the sun even unto the going down of the same My name, saith the Lord of Hosts, is great among the Gentiles, and in every place there is sacrifice, and there is offered to My name a *clean* oblation."

At last there was a pause, and the bishop turned round and faced the people. His presence was not at all imposing, and his tenor voice, though clear, did not at first indicate the orator or man of power. My first impression was one of disappointment. But this was momentary. The bishop spoke in a conversational tone. He was merely talking; but he had not spoken a minute before we discovered that it was the talk of a man of intellect, of culture, and deep thought; and we imagined from the line of his talk that he knew of our presence, and endeavored "to speak to our condition." I well remember how, in speaking of the completeness of Catholic doctrine, he said that even the humblest Catholic, who was well instructed in the catechism, had an immense advantage over even the most learned outsider or non-Catholic, because the Catholic stood, as it were, at the centre of truth, whence he could look out in all directions; while even the most learned non-Catholic stood as it were on a mere point on the outside of the circle, and could see only a short distance above or beyond on the circumference—the difference between outsiders being that the greatest or most learned man could see just a little further around than the others. And then the bishop went on to speak of the conquests that this Catho-

lic truth was making, mentioning the
then quite recent conversion of Dr. Newman and other Puseyites in England, and
the great philosopher, Dr. Brownson, and
others in this country—all of whom had
sought this central truth, and were happy
in having gained the illumination of its
glorious light.   Somehow, while this
grand utterance of the bishop struck
home to my soul, still I evaded its force
by fancying that our branch of the Church
was just as near the centre of truth as the
Papal or Roman Church.   And this illu-
sion continued with me yet for some
time.

Another incident to which I may allude was connected with the spirit-rap-
pings which were exceedingly prevalent
in 1845 and thereafter.   It was probably
due to something I had read in Brownson's writings that I was led to hold that
these or some of them were manifesta-

tions of evil spirits, with which it was just as wicked for the Christian to have intercourse as it was for King Saul to consult the Witch of Endor. It was a curious fact that very many, if not the majority, of the rapidly increasing multitude of Spiritists were people who were not noted for any religious belief; and yet here they were accepting without question belief in the agency of spirits which they knew nothing about, and had no means of determining whether they were good or bad. The more this matter of spirits was discussed the more I came to see how utterly inadequate and barren was the Protestant teaching respecting the agency of good angels among us. As to the consoling and comforting Catholic teaching in regard to our Guardian Angels,*

---

*The Catholic idea of the Guardian Angel is appropriately and beautifully expressed in the following prayer, which I copy for the benefit of my Prot-

I had never heard of it, or at least it had never been taught as a thing which we ought to believe.　And I well remember the surprise and pleasure with which I

———————

estant or non-Catholic readers, if there should be any :

A Prayer to One's Guardian Angel.

O most faithful companion, appointed by God to be my guardian, my protector, and defender, and who never leavest my side ; how shall I thank thee for thy faithfulness and love, and for all the benefits which thou hast conferred upon me?　Thou watchest over me while I sleep ; thou comfortest me when I am sad ; thou liftest me up when I am down ; thou avertest the dangers that threaten me ; thou warnest me of those that are to come ; thou withdrawest me from sin, and excitest me to good ; thou exhortest me to penance when I fall, and reconcilest me to God.　Long ago should I have been lost unless by thy prayers thou hadst turned away from me the anger of God.　Leave me not, nor forsake me ever, I beseech thee ; but still comfort me in adversity, restrain me in prosperity, defend me in danger, assist me in temptations, lest at any time I fall beneath them.　Offer up in the sight of the Divine Majesty my prayers and groanings, and all my works of piety, and make me to persevere in grace, until I come to everlasting life.　Amen.

read a remarkable passage in a book by Frederika Bremer, in the days when her books were so popular, contrasting the barrenness of belief of the people of her day in this regard, and their consequent low, dry, and narrow views of life, with that of their ancestors who were conscious of being surrounded with a world of Guardian Angels—of good spirits, and also of evil spirits, and to whom it was natural to live in a bright world of imagination teeming with beautiful and soul-inspiring legends.

It was also about this time—perhaps in 1849—that an Episcopal clergyman from another diocese, during a visit in my family where he found sympathetic listeners, advanced the idea that the Mother of our Divine Lord must necessarily have been a woman of *perfect* purity, and entitled to the highest possible honor and veneration. This struck me at once as being so reasonable that I thereafter wholly rejected the absurd Protestant charges against Catholics of Mariolatry. And I fully sympathized in this regard with the venerable Bishop Philander Chase (uncle of Chief-Justice Chase), who, after many years of separation, once more met a certain Episcopal minister who, in the mean time, had printed a book to show that the blessed virgin mother of Our Lord was the mother of other children; and when the minister advanced to greet him, the old bishop, in the dignity of his magnificent presence, repelled him with the scornful remark, "You beast!" It is needless to add that a little later on I had no difficulty whatever in accepting the dogma of the Immaculate Conception promulgated in 1854 by Pope Pius IX., of glorious memory.

A few words on another matter and then I shall come to the culminating point in my progress to Rome. Perhaps no prejudice was more deeply imbedded in my mind than that of the corruption of the Catholic Church in practice, as well as its defection in doctrine. And for a long time the argument against its claims to authority seemed to me to be fair and strong that God would not select and trust such a corrupt body to act as His favored instrument for the promulgation of His truth, and the administration of spiritual affairs on earth. I cannot now recall what author it was who gave a fatal shock to this assumption by citing the example of the Jewish Church, which, with all the errors and crimes of its priests, and the dreadful backslidings of its stiff-necked people, still remained the chosen Church of God, so that even Our Saviour Himself, when He had healed the leper, said to him: "Go, show thyself to the priest and offer for thy cleansing the things that Moses commanded for a testimony to them." Thus it dawned upon me that the agents whom God selects for the execution of His divine purposes are not guaranteed against erroneous conduct, nor even against the commission of sin, but are left, as were Lucifer, the brightest archangel, and Adam, with his lofty intelligence, to the exercise of their free will. And this reasonable view of the case went on enlarging until I learned that even the Pope, although infallible when speaking *ex cathedra* on a question of faith or morals, is not impeccable; that, as every intelligent person knows, or ought to know, his infallibility does not include or imply impeccability; and that, although he is the successor of St. Peter, and the head of the Church, with its two hundred and fifty millions of people, yet even he is obliged to go down on his knees before his confessor the same as the humblest lay-man.

Thus I have indicated how, from time to time, my views and prejudices were greatly modified and softened on a number of important points pertaining to church questions. And yet I continued to flatter myself that we high church *illuminati*, who had picked out the first four councils as our standards, and had settled it that St. Paul had founded the Anglican Church in Britain, could safely stand upon the branch theory—assuming that the Anglican Church (from which the American Episcopal Church derived its life) was as really a branch of the true Church as was the Church of Rome, or the Greek Church (for we held *that* also to be a true branch). In the midst of the distractions of business and politics which absorbed my attention, I know not how much longer I might have rested on this

6

frail assumption, when suddenly, like an electric shock, there came to me an epistle from my brother, who was spending the winter of 1849–50 in New Orleans for his health, containing these startling words: "I am a Roman Catholic in belief." Of course I was astounded. But even the long exposition and argument set forth in his letter did not convince me; and I still felt sure that if I only had the time and opportunity I could demonstrate to his satisfaction that the Anglican Church was the true *via media* and house of refuge, avoiding, as I imagined, the disintegrating individualism of Protestantism on the one hand, and what I then considered the liberty-killing absolutism of the Papacy on the other hand.

In the heat and enthusiasm of his new conviction, my brother soon returned to his home in Columbus, expecting to carry with him to Rome a number of his devoted high church friends. But he soon found that he had reckoned without his host. His advances were met with horror and indignation. And the storm of opposition was such that he was fain to bend under it for a time till the gale should be overpast. Of course he was not inclined to do any more preaching, and indeed the state of his health furnished a good excuse for his silence. Yet during this intermediate state of nearly two years—the unhappiest of his life—he did preach a few times, and he produced one sermon which he delivered at Gambier—doubtless with a grim sort of pleasure—before the professors, theological students, and *literati* of Kenyon College and Bexley Hall, causing a buzz and fermentation that lasted for some time, and leaving the impression that he too was well along on the road to Rome.

Not long thereafter he delivered the same sermon in our church in Newark. I noticed it particularly because it showed that he had familiarized himself with the idea that the Church is a visible corporation, an organic body with a life and head of its own. Speaking of the popular error of making the preaching of faith everything, he said: "It is not belief merely that imparts spiritual life. We must come into organic connection with Christ the Head. As the individual is united to the head of the race by natural generation, so he is united to the Head of the Church by spiritual regeneration. The life of Christianity is a corporate life. God has chosen to provide means by which children shall be new-born to Him by a principle of continuity and reproduction which makes them all one, binds them together in one body, and through that body to the one Head, even

Christ. Thus the Church is a visible, organized body. The God-man has taken it into union with Himself. He has breathed upon it the divine effluence. The Holy Ghost has taken up His abode in it, and the God-man has promised to be with it to the end of time."

This quotation will suffice to show the drift of his thought. He had closely observed the controversy in 1844 between Dr. Seabury and Dr. Brownson, and had specially noticed, as I had not, that Seabury, although invited by Brownson to do so, had never replied to Brownson's October article in which he argued and proved, in reply to Seabury, that the Anglican Church was schismatic. Seabury had admitted, with the Oxford divines, that the Church was a corporation. But he seemed to think he had raised up an effectual guard by asserting that a "visible centre" and a "visible head"

were *not* essential to the existence of a
corporate body.   To this Brownson answered by quoting abundant authority to
show that, while the *right* of a number of
persons to act collectively as a corporation is invisible, yet the corporation itself is as visible a body as an army.   In
like manner the *authority* of the Church is
invisible; for it is the authority of Christ,
who is its invisible Head.   But the individuals composing the corporation, and
the organs through which it acts, are
visible; and this, Brownson said, was all
the visibility he contended for.   And
then taking the Oxford divines on their
own principle—that the Church is a corporation — Brownson   held   that   "the
Church must needs be one in the unity of
the corporation, and one in its corporate
authority, as well as one in the unity of
faith and charity.   Now if the Church be
a single body, corporate or politic, as it

must be if it is one corporation, and not an assemblage of corporations, then the Anglicans, in breaking the unity of the corporation, as we all know they did, were guilty of schism." And "the Church of England" being a "distinct, independent polity, participating in the *authority* of no other body, but holding communion with the authority of no body but itself, is, therefore, not a *member* of the Catholic body." It is cut off—schismatic.

Such was the argument of a portion of Brownson's October article, to which Seabury made no reply, as my brother had noticed, and the force and truth of which he had admitted in his own mind, although he was delaying to act out his convictions. As he did not, in his sermon—which we called his "organic sermon"—go on to argue with Brownson that the Anglican Church was schismatic,

I most heartily indorsed his theory of the Church as an organic body, but I was not yet quite ready to take the last step. While writing this address I learned from him that at the time when he wrote that sermon, his mind was greatly impressed with the following syllogism: "Every organized body must have a head. The Church is an organized body. Therefore the Church must have a head." This brings to mind Father Hecker's mention, in his "Aspirations of Nature," of the case of a celebrated professor of natural history * who, years ago, called on the Bishop of Philadelphia, and in a state of evident excitement bluntly asked the bishop: "Sir! do you know of any reason why I should not become a Catholic?" "On the contrary," answered the bishop, "I know of many reasons why you

---

* Professor Haldemann.

should." Having come to a good understanding, the bishop, finding that the
professor was in earnest, asked him what
it was that first directed his thoughts to
Catholic doctrine. "Bugs! Bugs!" was
the prompt answer. "Bugs," repeated
the astonished bishop, "what have these
to do with the truth of the Catholic religion?" And then the professor related
how he discovered one day by the aid of
a microscope that a family of animalculæ
had a perfect system of an organized government—with a chief and subordinate
officers, all acting in unison and perfect
order. This unexpected discovery led
the professor to make other observations,
when he found everywhere in the wide
field of nature the same law, the same
form of government, from the meanest
floweret or insect to the vast system of
worlds. And then it occurred to him
that this same system of order and gov-

ernment prevailed also in God's spiritual
government.   And then he sought a
Catholic bishop, and found his proper
home in the Catholic Church.

In this matter of the headship my
brother had got a little ahead of me in his
progress on the road to Rome, although
halting for a brief period.   But it required one more impulse, one more thun-
der-clap, so to speak, to rouse us both to
the last effort, and that came in a short
time to my brother, in the month of
November, 1851, in the guise of sickness
almost unto death.   Then he called for a
Catholic priest that he might be recon-
ciled to the Church and make his peace
with God at once.   His request was denied.   Then there was a commotion in
his wide family circle by marriage.   And
it was in the midst of the excitement
which followed that I went from Newark to Columbus to visit him.   Acting as

a peacemaker, I was happy to see that
the excitement was temporarily allayed,
and I arranged that he should visit me at
my quiet home at Newark just as soon as
he could safely get out.   In a short time
this plan was carried out—my expecta-
tion being that in the peace and quietness
of my home his excitement would pass
away, and that by calmly reasoning together we would harmonize, as we always
had done, and meet again on the good
old *via media*.   Little did I anticipate the
unanswerable arguments for the Catholic
Church which he had already mastered,
and with which he unexpectedly but
effectually posed me.

Among other points presented by him,
it would be well worth a half hour's lecture to quote the texts from the New
Testament which he cited and showed
had either never received any interpretation, or had been grossly misinterpreted

by Protestants, such as: "Thou art Peter
(a rock) and upon this rock I will build
My Church, and the gates of hell shall
never prevail against it"; and especially
passages in the sixth chapter of John.
But time does not permit this now, and I
must hasten on to say that my brother's
quiet visit to me was soon ended, with
benefit to his physical health, but with no
such change as I·expected in his spiritual
condition.   When he returned home he
lost no time in seeing a priest (Father
Borgess, afterward Bishop of Detroit),
and in being received into the Church on
the festival of the conversion of St. Paul,
January 25, 1852.*

---

*In his letter to *The Catholic Columbian*, of
Columbus, Ohio, dated January 25, 1892, and afterward published at St. Paul, Minn., in Pamphlet
No. 29 of "The Catholic Truth Society of America,"
under the title, "Forty Years in the Church," he paid
this fervent tribute to the Church in this eloquent
passage:

"For forty years I have been studying the Catholic

I have thought it proper and needful to mention these few details by way of introduction to the climax in my own progress to Rome. For our interviews at various times, before, during, and after that visit of my brother resulted in the discussion of the question of authority, and on that matter I could not gainsay his experience as an Episcopal minister in the various diocesan and triennial conventions which he had attended during

---

Church, both theoretically and practically—its system of teaching, of devotion, and its wonderful organization ; and I must say its magnitude, its beauty, and its glory have grown upon me continually till I am ready to declare that there is nothing like it in all the world. It bears unmistakable evidence of the divinity of its origin and the superhuman wisdom of its organization and development. The only wonder is that a system so grand, so venerable, so fraught with all that is intellectually great and devotionally beautiful and attractive should not have commanded more attention from intellectual men, and more general investigation of claims whose proof lies as it were on the surface, and is so easily accessible to any candid, honest inquirer."

the previous ten years, and at the close
of all of which he found himself and his
Church just as far as ever from an authoritative settlement of a number of "controversies of faith" which went to the
very essence and foundation of Christianity.   Ranging from the lowest low
churchman to the highest high churchman, the variations of doctrine and views
held by them were numerous, startling,
irreconcilable.   In vain had we looked,
lo! these many years, for a realization by
the Episcopal Church of its famous assertion "that the Church hath authority in
controversies of faith."   No such authority had we been able to find in the Episcopal Church.

And yet the conviction had grown in
us to the force of a burning truth that
that authority must exist and reside
somewhere in a visible, tangible, recog-
nizable form, or else Revelation was a

sham, the Church a delusion, the world simply chaos, and human life not worth living! For it all came to this, as was once said by an old Presbyterian minister, that God having seen fit to create man with reason and free will, it is due to that creature that means should be provided whereby he may infallibly know what is the will, the law of God, which the creature must obey. Is it reasonable to require man to obey a law under pain of losing his soul, and yet to leave things in such a loose way that no man can ever be *certain* as to what that law is?

Here is the grand, central starting point. Settle this, and all other questions which we need to have settled will settle themselves. Let the Catholic always hold his antagonist rigidly to this point until it is settled. If accepted, agreement will readily follow. If rejected, controversy is almost useless, especially on questions of interpretation and history, because there is no mutually accepted judge to decide, and no mutually accepted standard by which to be governed. If then it is *due* to the creature that means should be provided whereby he may infallibly know the law of God so far as it pertains to man's eternal salvation, it follows that these means have been provided. For what God *ought* to do, He certainly does not fail to do. And if He has provided the means spoken of, then we must be able to find them readily. For if we cannot find and identify them, they might just as well *not* have been provided, and the result must be uncertainty, anarchy, chaos. Therefore they must be open, visible, ascertainable, so that even he who runs may read, and the wayfaring man though a fool may understand.

As already indicated by quotations from

my Kenyon oration, I had even then out-grown the common Protestant notion—so deeply and almost ineradicably implanted in the Protestant mind—that the Bible contains the whole counsel and will of God, and that each one must go to that fountain for the rule of faith. I had asked then, as I ask now: "Does the Bible interpret itself?" As well might one ask: "Does the volume of statutes issued every year by Congress interpret itself? Does Congress throw out that book and say to each citizen: 'There is the law of the land; read it and find out for yourself what it means'?" How long would it be before the nation would be reduced to hopeless and destructive anarchy on that scheme? To save the nation from this terrible result, Congress has, under the Constitution, established the Supreme Court of the United States to interpret the laws and decide between

7

disputants. And this court is an authority outside and independent of each one, to be recognized, respected, and obeyed by each one.

Now is not the spiritual superior to the temporal? Is not the soul above the body? Are not the things that concern the eternal welfare of the soul of more importance than the mere temporal interests that concern this short span of life? If then the Bible contains the will of God concerning the salvation of man, must it not be interpreted? For, observe, this will or law of God is and must be one and the same for all men, in all times; and its interpreter must be some one having authority objective to each man, above each man, and imperative upon all men. This view, as a matter of course, excludes that other popular Protestant assumption that God makes known His will by a special revelation to each one; for this would virtually constitute each one an authority, not only for himself, but for every one else. Certainly no one can establish so absurd a proposition; for how could you prove to me that you had had such a special revelation; or how could I prove to you that I had? Plainly there never could be in this way a common objective standard outside of each one, independent of each one, and yet authoritative for all. Therefore it follows that authority must be lodged somewhere outside of yourself, outside of myself, and yet accessible to all and ascertainable by all.

Where then is this authority lodged? Is it to be supposed that Our Saviour, while fulfilling His mission on earth, overlooked this matter? How then did He arrange it? Of course, while yet on earth His word was law to His disciples. Did He not also intend that word to be the law to all men in all times? And how

was that law to be made known to men
except through His disciples? Therefore
He commissioned them to go into all the
world and teach all nations. And, strange
to say, He did not give them even *one*
book of the New Testament to start out
with. And it is a historical fact that the
latest book of the New Testament was
not even written till about the last year
of the First Century, and the Bible itself
was not collected and authenticated by
the Church in its official capacity for
more than three hundred years after the
Ascension. And yet during those three
hundred years and more, did not the
apostles and their authorized successors
teach the word, the law of God? How
came they to know it infallibly, and that
too for a long time without any *written*
word? For even the liturgy, as stated
by Father Thébaud in his great work on
the Church, although composed, was not

written for many years after the Ascension, and during the first century, at least, every priest had to commit to memory the formulas of prayers, rites, and ceremonies. Not even the Creed and *Pater Noster* were put on paper or parchment. The catechumens had to learn them by word of mouth from their teachers, as well as everything else connected with religion.*

---

*The apostles and their immediate successors were familiar with the custom of the oral transmission of religious traditions which prevailed in the sacred colleges of the Jews, the Romans, the Egyptians, and the Brahmans. A striking example of this custom was given by Professor Whitney in his learned article on "The Veda" in *The Century* for April, 1887, in which, speaking of the Vedic songs, he says: " There are more than a thousand of these songs, and they contain over ten thousand two-line stanzas—a body of text about equal to the two Homeric poems taken together." The professor gave it as his opinion that this collection of Vedic hymns dates from about two thousand years before Christ, and he said that "this great mass of literature"—including all the Vedas—"has been handed down to our time mainly

Now was not all this work done in the
mode prescribed by Our Lord? He promised that the Holy Spirit should guide His
disciples into the truth. When, therefore, they taught what God required of
men to believe and to do in order to be
saved, how could they be certain of
teaching God's will infallibly unless they
were certainly guided by the Holy Spirit?
Yet they could not teach a common doctrine without agreement, and they could
not agree without consultation, discus-

---

by living tradition, from the mouth of the teacher to
the ear of the scholar.   The schools of the Brahman
priesthood . . . are not yet extinct. There is not one
of the Vedic texts which has not still in India its personal representatives, men who, without ever having seen a manuscript of it, can repeat it from beginning to end, with all its tones and accents, and not
losing a syllable."

In the same way the Creed, the prayers, the Canon
of the Mass, the hymns, the Psalms, and the ancient
music to which they were sung, were all known and
transmitted by the apostles to their catechumens and
their successors.

sion, and a final embodiment of the truth to be taught in a "form of sound words." Thus acted in concert that body—the Church—organized by Our Lord to last till the end of time. The officers of that organic body, having authority to act derived from Our Lord, were infallibly guided into the expression of truth when they formulated definitions of faith; that is, prescribed what it was necessary to believe and to do in order to be saved. And the grand reason why men are bound to accept these definitions is precisely because the Holy Spirit guides the Church, and especially the head of the Church—the successor of St. Peter *—

---

* In the fall of 1853, while spending several weeks in Columbus, engaged on some literary work, I visited in the family of Isaac N. Whiting, and was urged, by way of arresting my progress to Rome, to read the work of Bishop Barrow on the "Supremacy of the Pope." I took the volume which was hope fully handed me, and undertook to read it. I well

into all necessary truth.   Thus it is God Himself who speaks to us through these definitions, made and delivered to men authoritatively in this way.   Here is divine authority acting through human instrumentalities.   Here is our certainty; here is our security.   We know in whom we believe, and we know what we believe.   I am just as certain that a dogma of the Church contains the truth and expresses the will of God, as I am that God exists.   There is and there can be no error and no mistake in these dogmas.

---

remember the interest with which I read the chapter in which the bishop quoted every verse in the New Testament containing the name of Peter, and I was not surprised at his full admission that of the apostles Peter was *primus inter pares*.   But the bishop's subsequent argument against the supremacy of Peter struck me as being about on a par with the argument of Presbyterians against the Episcopacy, which I had long since decided was illogical and untenable.   And so my progress to Rome was not arrested, but, on the contrary, was rather hastened.

And not a single instance can be found in the whole history of the Church of one dogma contradicting another. You might just as well expect that the All-Wise God would reveal one thing to-day, and a totally contradictory thing to-morrow.

Now it is a matter of history that this Church was organized and instructed, and the doctrines of Christ were preached, and branches of the Church were established in all parts of the Roman Empire, in Persia and Bactriana, in far India and parts of China, and it is highly probable that St. Thomas even visited Central America, before the latest book of the New Testament was written. And it was this Church, acting officially, that passed judgment upon the numerous gospels, epistles, and other writings which were claimed to be sacred scriptures, and rejected many, and selected what now constitute the canon of Holy Scripture. And that Church is now, always has been, and always will be, during this dispensation, the living interpreter of that book, as well as the interpreter of divine revelation outside of that book—the keeper and witness of the truth. Consequently when a question arises involving faith or morals—things necessary to be believed or to be done in order to be saved—the first duty is to inquire, "What does the Church teach?" When the Church, or the head of the Church, speaks *ex cathedra*, I must accept its definition just as I would accept a direct and properly attested revelation from God. I must also accept its teaching within the domain of discipline and official instruction.

But all beyond that domain and the dogmas of the Church, which by the way can readily be enumerated—some of the most important being: God, the Trinity, the Incarnation, Transubstantiation, the Fall of Man, the Hypostatic Union, the Seven Sacraments, the Immaculate Conception, and the Infallibility of the Pope —I say all beyond these and the domain referred to is free ground, is the region of opinion in which the widest freedom is allowed consistent with those fundamental truths; a freedom that is all the more perfect and satisfactory because we can start out from that centre of truth which I heard Bishop Purcell describe as radiating principles of absolute certainty in every direction, which serve at once as chart, compass, and anchor, with a beacon light forever illuminated by the glorious light from Heaven.

Without this interpreter, thus divinely aided and guided, who could have formulated with certainty and established the doctrines of the Trinity, the Incarnation, Transubstantiation, and all the other great truths of Christianity? But *with* this interpreter, and the definitions which it unerringly makes, and the traditions which it unerringly preserves and transmits, the humblest layman may find the truth with certainty, and the honest seeker after truth, however long in wandering mazes lost, and however fiercely storm-tossed upon the ragged edge of those questions of destiny which perplex and agitate the souls of non-Catholics, may easily find, as I found in the summer of 1853, a port of safety, a harbor of rest, and that sublime peace of soul which passes all understanding—a peace which is based upon the believer's absolute conviction and certainty that the dogmas and points of faith of the Church flow logically from belief in God, thus verifying the famous saying of the French philosopher, Proudhon, who thought he was an atheist, but said: "Admit God, and the

Roman Catholic Church, with its dogmas, is the logical consequence."

"Admit God!" As if a man of any sense could do otherwise. On this point let me say a word. Obviously all my remarks have assumed the existence of God, and have been addressed to those who admit it. What then can I say to those unfortunate persons who assent to the assertion of agnostics that you cannot prove God, and therefore relegate that idea to the region of the "unknowable"? My answer shall be given in a few words from Dr. Brownson, who, in 1873, said:* "Though reason is competent to prove the existence of God with certainty when denied or doubted, as we think we have shown, it did not, and perhaps could not, have originated the idea, but has taken it from tradition, and it

---

* Works, vol. ii., p. 97.

must have been actually taught the first man by his Maker Himself." "If," then, as Brownson said in his review of William Francis Newman's essay on the soul,* "the human mind is unable to generate the belief in God," and "if we can have it only as we are taught it, we must either assume that God Himself has first taught us, or else suppose an infinite series of teachers. Your father may have taught you, but who taught him? His father. But who taught his father? These questions may be continued to infinity, and we must either assert an infinite series of teachers, which is an infinite absurdity, or we must stop with the first man, the commencement of the series of generations, and then arises the question, Who taught the first man? God Himself, is the only answer conceiv-

---

* Works, vol. i., p. 265.

able, and then God really is; for if He were not, He could not teach His existence, since what is not cannot act. This is historically the way in which the belief has actually originated. God taught the first man His own existence, and the belief has been perpetuated to us by the unbroken chain of tradition." Thus the human race came into possession of the idea and has never lost it, and never will lose it. Therefore it was true in the days of old, and it is true to-day, that only the fool hath said in his heart there is no God. Furthermore the very fact of the existence in the mind of man of the *idea* of God, as argued by St. Anselm and Brownson, is unanswerable proof of the existence of God.*

---

* At last that famous "unknowable" theory, which during the last twenty years or more has played so conspicuous a part in the writings of "scientists," and has exerted such a widespread demoralizing in-

I may here appropriately add the remark of Father Faber, in regard to the

---

fluence in all "civilized" society, has itself been hap-
pily relegated to the region of darkness from which
it came.   For confirmation I refer to two remarkable articles—one, the profoundly scientific and criti-
cal address of Lord Salisbury, president of the Brit-
ish Association, at its last annual meeting (see
Popular Science Monthly for November, 1894), and
the other, the no less profound and learned article in
the *Revue des Deux Mondes* for January, 1895,
headed "After a Visit to the Vatican," written by the
editor, M. Ferdinand Brunetière, embodying his re-
flections suggested by his interview with the Pope on
the 27th of November, 1894, when the principal subject was the question, "How far has the advance of
science crowded out religious faith?"   After pointing
out the "bankruptcy of science" in its failure to re-
deem its promises to furnish man with the *only* means
he has for ameliorating his lot, the editor said, as
translated and digested by *The Literary Digest :*

"No one can deny that the physical or natural
sciences have promised to suppress 'mystery.'   Not
only have they not suppressed it, but we see clearly
to-day that they never will throw light on it.   They
are powerless—I will not say to resolve, but even to
give a hint of a solution of questions of the utmost
importance to us : these are the questions relating to
the origin of man, the law of his conduct, and his
future destiny.   The unknowable surrounds us, en-

idea of the Incarnation, that neither men
nor angels—"not even the highest an-

---

velops us, constrains us; and we cannot get from the
laws of physics or the results of physiology any
means of knowing anything about this unknowable.
I admire as much as anybody the immortal labors of
Darwin. . . . Yet, whether we are descended from
the monkey, or the monkey and ourselves have a
common ancestor, we have not advanced a step
toward knowing anything about the origin of man.
Neither anthropology, nor ethnology, nor linguistics,
has ever been able to tell us *what we are.* What is
the origin of language? What is the origin of society? What is the origin of morality? Whoever
[evidently meaning the scientists referred to], in
this century, has tried to answer these questions has
failed miserably. And every one [of the same class]
who hereafter shall try to answer these questions
will fail as miserably, because you cannot conceive
of man without morality, without language, or outside of society; and thus the very elements of the
solutions are beyond the reach of science.

.   .   .   .

"It is clear that the fact that science, after long
trying, has been unable to aid us in any way in *living
properly* has been recognized by a great multitude of
persons. This is proved unmistakably by the literature of the last few years. There has been an un-
deniable change in the sentiments of both writers
and readers. The present situation may be summed

S

gelical intelligence could have conceived it without a revelation from God; and Scripture pictures the angels to us as ever bending over and looking into this mystery to feed their love, their wisdom, and their adoration out of its depths of glory and sweetness."

That remarkable and glorious title of Our Lord—"The Angel of the Great Council"—derives its significance from that one of the councils of eternity characterized by the decree of the Incarnation, which, as many theologians teach, preceded the permission of sin, was the first act of the Trinity *ad extra*—outside of itself, and was the beginning of all creation, as declared by St. John in that magnificent opening of his gospel: "In the beginning was the Logos—the Word,

----

up in a very few words: Science has lost its *prestige*, and religion has reconquered a part of its own."

and the Word was with God, and the Word was God. The same was in the beginning with God. All things were made by Him, and without Him was made nothing that was made"—the angels, the countless worlds, and man himself. And thus, as Father Faber says in "The Blessed Sacrament" (Book IV., Section III.): "The Incarnation lies at the bottom of all sciences, and is their ultimate explanation. It is the secret beauty in all arts. It is the completeness of all true philosophies. It is the point of arrival and departure to all history. The destinies of nations, as well as of individuals, group themselves around it. It purifies all happiness, and glorifies all sorrow. . . . It is the great central fact both of life and immortality, out of sight of which man's intellect wanders in the darkness, and the light of a divine life falls not on his footsteps.

"There never has been in the world a power like to this power of the Incarnation. None which has wrought such changes, or brought about such tremendous revolutions. None which has gathered to itself such enthusiastic loyalty, or for which men have been so eager to lay down their lives and to shed their blood. None which has allured such a vast amount of holiness to adorn it, or of consummate intelligence to propagate and defend it."

And yet "the Incarnation is not simply a past fact; it is the living life of the Incarnate God. It is not merely the glory of the theological schools; it is the *sacrifice of the daily altar*. On earth as well as in heaven, Jesus Himself is the present centre round which all the elements of the world of the Incarnation are perpetually revolving. . . . Nothing will explain the phenomena of the Church, nothing will interpret its history, or account for its miraculous propagation and preservation, except the *Blessed Sacrament.*" As it is the life of the Church, so is it the life of the individual, and becomes to every worthy communicant the seed of immortality whereby the lost image of the Word made flesh is restored to man, and the perfection of his nature is realized by participation in the divine life.

When at last I saw the truth, I could well exclaim with St. Augustine: "O Eternal Truth! Ever ancient and ever new! Too late have I known Thee! Too late have I loved Thee!"

[PRINTED BY BENZIGER BROTHERS, NEW YORK.]

www.ingramcontent.com/pod-product-compliance
Lightning Source LLC
Chambersburg PA
CBHW032019010726
47493CB00007B/2484